THE THREE
Little Pugs

1 Moldylocks and
the Three Beards

2 Little Red
Quacking Hood

Read more of Princess Pink's adventures!

3 The Three
Little Pugs

4 Jack and
the Snackstalk

Princess Pink AND THE LAND OF FAKE-BELIEVE

THE THREE Little Pugs

by Noah Z. Jones

BRANCHES

SCHOLASTIC INC.

FOR THE PUGLIEST SIBLINGS I KNOW: NATHAN, EMILY, AND ZOE

Copyright © 2015 by Noah Z. Jones

All rights reserved. Published by Scholastic Inc.,
Publishers since 1920. SCHOLASTIC, BRANCHES, and associated logos are trademarks and/or registered trademarks of Scholastic Inc.

The publisher does not have any control over and does not assume any responsibility for author or third-party websites or their content.

Library of Congress Cataloging-in-Publication Data included below
Jones, Noah (Noah Z.), author.
The three little pugs / by Noah Z. Jones. — First edition.
pages cm. — (Princess Pink and the Land of Fake-Believe ; 3)
Summary: In the Land of Fake-Believe the Three Little Pugs' used car business has sold Scaredy-Pants Wolf a lemon (literally) instead of a delivery van, so Princess Pink gets an opportunity to use her karate moves to get Wolf's money back— and set the Pugs on the straight-and-narrow path to business success.
ISBN 0-545-84857-1 (pbk.) — ISBN 0-545-84858-X (hardcover) — ISBN 0-545-84859-8 (ebook) — ISBN 0-545-84860-1 (eba ebook)
1. Fairy tales. 2. Wolves—Juvenile fiction. 3. Pug—Juvenile fiction. 4. Used car trade—Juvenile fiction. 5. Lemon—Juvenile fiction. 6. Humorous stories. [1. Fairy tales. 2. Humorous stories. 3. Wolves—Fiction. 4. Pug—Fiction. 5. Dogs—Fiction.] I. Title.
PZ8.J539Th 2015
[Fic]—dc23
2014041916

10 9 8 7 6 5 4 3 2 1   15 16 17 18 19/0

Printed in the U S A.   23
First Scholastic printing, September 2015

Edited by Katie Carella
Book design by David DeWitt

◆ TABLE OF CONTENTS ◆

· CHAPTER ONE ·
No Pink Tutus!

This is Princess Pink. Her first name is <u>Princess</u>. Her last name is <u>Pink</u>.

Princess does not like princesses or ballerinas. And she **REALLY** does not like the color pink.

Princess likes running and jumping and yelling at the top of her lungs. And she **REALLY** likes karate.

Princess's seven brothers like karate, too. But she is the karate champ!

That's my little kicker!

Princess broke another board and won a new belt! It was purple.

I can't stand purple! It's almost as bad as pink!

What if I break <u>two</u> boards? Then can I get the brown belt?

That night, Princess showed her new belt to her friend Reggie the spider. He crawled out from under her pillow.

Wow! Another belt?!

The rest of the Pink family did not know about Reggie. They also did not know that Princess took late-night trips through her refrigerator into the zany, mixed-up Land of Fake-Believe.

Princess sneaked down to the kitchen.

She put the magnet on the fridge.
Then she turned it to the left—just like
Mother Moose had told her to do. A
blast of light filled the room. The fridge
stopped its usual <u>HUMMmmm</u> sound. It
began to sparkle and shine.

Princess tugged open the door. It was early morning in the Land of Fake-Believe. She saw what looked like Humpty Dumpty falling off a wall. Only he was tie-dyed.

Land of Fake-Believe, here I come!

Princess stepped inside her fridge.

Then she climbed down the ladder.

◆ CHAPTER TWO ◆
Big Bad Lemon

Princess quickly made her way to the Big Bad Bakery. She could see her friends Moldylocks and Scaredy-Pants Wolf through the window.

Princess opened the door. Moldylocks
rushed over. But she didn't hug Princess
hello. She pulled her inside.

Hey, Moldylocks!

I'm so glad you're here!
We really need your help!

As usual, Scaredy-Pants was crying as
he rolled out the dough for a pie.

Oh, hi, Princess!

BOO
HOO!

BOO
HOO!

Scaredy-Pants didn't stop crying. But he did offer Princess some pie.

BOO HOO!

Would you like a slice?

Not today. Thanks!

I've eaten enough wolf tears.

Moldylocks pulled Princess by the hand.

What's all the fuss about?

Scaredy-Pants has a big problem. Come on, we'll show you!

Moldylocks dragged Princess toward the garage. There, Scaredy-Pants Wolf filled her in on the whole story.

I needed a new van to deliver pies. So I tried to buy one from the Three Little Pugs. But the deal went sour! They sold me a lemon!

The Three Little Pugs tricked him. Look!

Princess looked inside the garage.

She expected to see a run-down delivery van. But instead she saw a lemon.

Was there a mix-up at the car dealership? Maybe the Pugs thought you needed a lemon for one of your pies?

I need a new van—not more pies! I'd like to ask for my money back. But those shady Pugs scare me.

I'm not afraid of small dogs. In fact, I kind of like pugs and their mushy, little faces!

I was hoping you'd say that, Princess! Let's go talk to them!

Don't worry, Scaredy-Pants! We'll get this sorted out.

Scaredy-Pants stayed at the bakery with his very pricey lemon.

Princess and Moldylocks headed off to the Three Little Pugs's car lot.

As soon as they got there, the Three Little Pugs tried to sell them a car.

THREE LITTLE PUGS
SALE

Welcome, ladies! <u>Ooh</u>, that hair. Fabulous. I have just the right color car for you. It's pink! You're going to love it!

Princess and Moldylocks were too smart for the Three Little Pugs.

The Three Little Pugs knew they were in trouble. They made a run for it.

Then they sped off in their SUV.

Princess and Moldylocks ran down the lane after the Three Little Pugs.

· CHAPTER THREE ·
House of Straws

Princess and Moldylocks jogged all the way to the First Little Pug's house. It was made out of drinking straws.

The girls caught their breath. Then Princess knocked on the door.

Little Pug, little Pug, let us in!

Before Princess had a chance to kick her way in, the First Little Pug opened the door.

Princess held up a picture of Scaredy-Pants Wolf.

This is our friend.
He wanted a van.
But you sold him a lemon.

We're here to get
his money back.

29

The First Little Pug was angry. He was <u>so</u> angry that he slammed the door. And he slammed the door <u>so</u> hard that the entire house of straws crashed to the ground!

The First Little Pug climbed into his SUV. Princess and Moldylocks couldn't chase after him—they were buried under lots of straws.

A large piece of paper flew out of the Pug's sunroof as he sped off. Princess jumped up to catch it.

Look at this!

What is it?

Princess and Moldylocks took a closer look.

It's a map of Fake-Believe.

What are all these red X marks?

I don't know. But these sneaky Pugs must be up to something.

We need to find out what!

Princess tucked the map into her pocket. Then the two friends ran off after the SUV.

Finally, Princess and Moldylocks found the First Little Pug's SUV. It was parked at his brother's house. The Second Little Pug's house was made out of fish sticks.

There's something fishy about this house.

The girls caught their breath. Then
Princess knocked loudly on the door.

No one answered. So Princess Pink
karate-chopped the door down.

HI-YAAHH!!!

The Second Little Pug came to what was left of the door. His brother stood behind him. They smiled at the girls.

Princess and Moldylocks were not sure if they should go inside.

The two Little Pugs politely pulled out chairs for the girls. Then they poured them each a cup of hot cocoa.

Marshmallows?

Yes, please.

Oh, dear. We forgot napkins. We'll be right back. Help yourself to some cookies.

The Pugs left the kitchen. Moldylocks saw a stack of napkins on the table.

Wait a second...

But it was too late.

Princess opened the cookie jar.

Snakes exploded out of the top! They drank up all the cocoa. They ate up all the marshmallows. Then they ate the whole house. There wasn't a single fishy crumb left. The entire house was gone.

Please don't eat us!

Hi! I'm Brian! Thanks for letting my buddies and me out of the cookie jar!

Um . . . you're welcome.

You see, the Three Little Pugs trapped us in there. And that was after they sold us a snake bus that turned out to be a real lemon and—

<u>VROOM</u>! Just then, a loud revving sound shook the ground.

The two Little Pugs were driving off in the biggest SUV Princess had ever seen.

Princess whistled. Soon, her old friend
Tunacorn flew in.

Who needs a car when
you have Tunacorn?!

Your tuna head doesn't
smell so bad after
all those fish sticks.

45

• CHAPTER FIVE •
House of Bricks

Princess and Moldylocks climbed on Tunacorn's back. It whisked the girls up, up, and away.

Tunacorn landed next to the Third Little Pug's house. It was made out of cheese bricks. Princess and Moldylocks climbed down.

Whoa! This cheese has been in the sun way too long.

Pee-yew! Even I don't like the smell of moldy cheese!

NOT WELCOME

The girls stomped up to the door
of the Third Little Pug's house. Then
Princess knocked with all her might.

49

No one answered. So Princess took
two steps back. Then she karate-kicked
the door.

Her foot got stuck in the cheese.

Moldylocks helped Princess get unstuck.

Then the girls heard a hissing noise. They turned to look and . . .

. . . they spotted a snake in the grass!
But it wasn't just any snake. It was
Brian—and his crew of snake buddies.

Hey! What are you doing here?

We came to finish
what we started.

Gulp! They
can't still
be hungry.
Can they?!

Please don't say you're
here to eat us!

No. No. No. We're here to
help you stop the Pugs.

Then Moldylocks had a crazy-cakes idea.

In no time at all, Brian and his buddies had tied up the Three Little Pugs. Brian opened the front door.

OUCH-A-MUNGA! These snakes have a tight squeeze!

We'll give you anything you want.

We promise to be good!

Start talking, Pugs! Why are you selling lemons and NOT cars?

The Three Little Pugs started talking.

We're just trying to make a living.

What are the Xs on this map?

The Xs are where we plan to build car lots. The Land of Fake-Believe is going to be our used car empire.

I wouldn't count on it.

We are **really** good at our job!

Princess tore up the map.

Brian found boxes and boxes of lemons in the basement. When Princess saw the lemons, she got an idea.

• CHAPTER SEVEN •
Payback Time!

Princess and Moldylocks put the Pugs to work.

Brian and his friends helped out.

Princess and Moldylocks ran all over Fake-Believe. They spread the word about the Pugs's new job.

If the Pugs tricked you, follow us!

Bring your lemon! The Pugs will give you your money back!

And come buy some tasty lemonade!

The Three Little Pugs finished setting up the lemonade stand.

HMPH! This is never going to work.

GRUMPH! No one makes money selling lemonade.

KERFLUMPH! This is a waste of time.

NO RETURNS OR EXCHANGES
LEMONADE SOLD AS IS

Finally, the store opened for business.

The lemonade stand had two lines.
One for buying fresh lemonade. And one
for returning lemons. The returns line
grew longer and longer.

Princess and Moldylocks watched the Three Little Pugs count up the money.

The Three Little Pugs paid everyone back. But they weren't done yet . . .

• CHAPTER EIGHT •
Keys to Happiness

The Pugs gave Scaredy-Pants Wolf a new delivery van.

Scaredy-Pants cried tears of joy. And the Three Little Pugs smiled. (But just a little.)

It's so shiny! I'm so happy!

Easy with the tears. You'll ruin my tie.

Boo Hoo!

"BIG BAD BAKERY

PUG$

Brian and his friends finally got their snake bus.

Then it was time for Princess Pink to head home.

69

Mother Moose and Tunacorn met
Princess and Moldylocks near the ladder
that led out of Fake-Believe.

We all owe you a <u>BIG</u> thank you!
Those Pugs fooled everyone.

Thanks for your help!

I'll be back soon!

Princess balanced the lemon pie as she
climbed up the ladder. Then she stepped
through her fridge.

Princess was SO tired. She dove into bed—and almost crushed Reggie.

Hey! Look out!

Sorry. Have some pie . . .

Noah Z. Jones

is an author, illustrator, and animator who creates all sorts of zany characters. He hopes this book will help kids learn to stay away from shifty pugs selling used cars! Noah has illustrated many books for children, including *Always in Trouble*, *Not Norman*, and *Those Shoes*. Princess Pink and the Land of Fake-Believe is the first children's book series that Noah has both written and illustrated.

How well do you know
THE LAND OF
FAKE-BELIEVE?

Why is Scaredy-Pants Wolf upset with the Three Little Pugs?

How does the Pugs's cookie jar trick end up helping Princess and her friends instead of hurting them?

How is the story of the **Three Little Pugs** similar to and different from the **Three Little Pigs**?

Use words and pictures to describe where each Little Pug lives. Which house would you want to live in?

Do you think Princess's plan to force the Three Little Pugs to pay back the money is fair? Why or why not?